JAMES RIORDAN is Professor of Languages and Academic Head of the Department of Linguistic and International Studies at the University of Surrey, a Fellow of the Royal Society for the Arts, and holds degrees from the universities of Birmingham, London and Moscow together with an honorary doctorate from L'Université de Stendhal, Grenoble. He has published over thirty volumes of collected folk tales, including *The Songs My Paddle Sings*, *The Woman in the Moon* and *The Barefoot Book of Stories from the Sea*. In 1968 he was awarded the Urals Peace Prize for *Mistress of the Copper Mountain*, and in 1996 *Great Uncle Tiger* was selected as a Children's Choice by the International Reading Association and the U.S. Children's Book Council. He regularly reviews children's books for *The Times*. His first book for Frances Lincoln was *The Twelve Labours of Hercules*.

JENNY STOW took her degree in English and History of Art in Manchester, going on to study at Chelsea School of Art. Between 1982 and 1985 she spent four years teaching in Africa, followed by a year in the Caribbean in 1987. Reviewing *The House that Jack Built*, her first book for Frances Lincoln, *Growing Point* wrote: 'Collectors of illustrative art should seize the book while they can.' Since then, Jenny has illustrated a series of four monster books written by John Agard (Longman Education), *Dark Fright* (Atheneum), and has written and illustrated *Growing Pains* for Frances Lincoln. She is married with one son.

About the story

The Yoruba live mainly on the coast of West Africa, especially in Nigeria, where they are the largest ethnic group. The Yoruba language is spoken by over 10 million people in the southwest of Nigeria.

Their historic kingdom dominated West Africa up to the 18th century. In Yoruba folklore, goddesses rule the pantheon of superior beings. Thus Ile is goddess of earth, Yemoja is goddess of water and her daughter Aje is goddess of the Niger River, from which Nigeria takes its name.

Versions of this traditional Yoruba tale can be found in a number of collections, including *West African Folktales* by William Barker, (Harrap, London, 1917); *Africa: Myths and Legends* by Alice Werner (Harrap, London, 1933); *Fourteen Hundred Cowrie: Traditional Stories of the Yoruba* by Abayomi Fuja (Oxford University Press, New York, 1964); *African Folktales* by Roger D. Abrahams (Pantheon Books, New York, 1983); *African Mythology* by Jan Knappert, (Diamond Books, London, 1995).

How to pronounce the names

Yemoya – *Yem-oy-ah*   Aje – *Eye-yeh*   Oduduwa – *O-doo-doo-wah*

For Chloe ～ J.R.

First published in Great Britain in 1999 by
Frances Lincoln Limited, 4 Torriano Mews
Torriano Avenue, London NW5 2RZ

First paperback edition 2000

British Library Cataloguing in Publication Data
available on request

ISBN 0-7112-1323-2 hardback
ISBN 0-7112-1378-X paperback

Set in Adminster

Printed in Hong Kong
1 3 5 7 9 8 6 4 2

The Coming of Night

A Yoruba Creation Myth
from West Africa

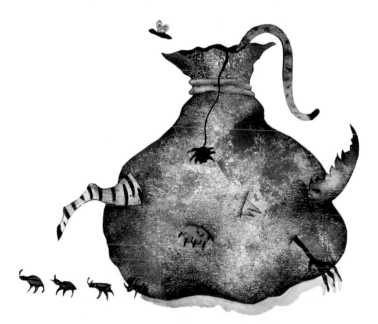

James Riordan
Illustrated by **Jenny Stow**

FRANCES LINCOLN

Long ago, when the earth was new,
it was forever day.

No moon, no stars, no night-hunting
owls and leopards.

No dawn to tell people when to rise,
no dusk to tell them when to sleep.

The land was bathed in bright sunshine
all the time.

One day, the great river goddess Yemoya
sent her daughter Aje to marry a handsome
earth chief, Oduduwa. Aje left her shady home
in the river's depths and went to live in the
Land of Shining Day.

At first, Aje was happy in her new home, and she loved her husband dearly. But after a while, she began to tire of the unrelenting sun. She told her husband, "This sunlight hurts my eyes. How I long for the cool shadows of my mother's home beneath the waves! How I wish that Night would come!"

Oduduwa was surprised.
"What is Night?" he asked.

"Night," said Aje wistfully,
"is a cool veil that curtains
the day's warm bed. It is the
gentle sigh that calms a restless
heart. It is the welcome rest
that refreshes a weary soul."

"Where is Night?"asked
Oduduwa.

"Only in my mother's
realm beneath the waves
can Night be found," said Aje.

At once the young chief went down to the river to talk
to Yemoya's messengers, Crocodile and Hippopotamus.
"Go to Yemoya," he said, "and ask her for Night.
Say it will make her daughter happy."

Crocodile and Hippopotamus dived into the watery depths.
They swam through the coral reefs, the gloomy caves
and dark grottoes. Finally, they came to a glittering palace.

Yemoya herself
came out to greet them.
   Bowing low before her,
they explained their mission:
her daughter longed for the shades of Night.
   Straight away, the goddess filled a sack
full of Night for them to take back to earth.
   "But heed my warning," Yemoya told them.
"Do not open the sack until you reach my
daughter. Only she can control the spirits of Night."

Swimming through the swirling waters, Crocodile
and Hippopotamus bore the sack between them until
they reached dry land. Once on the bank, they stopped
to rest and dry themselves in the sun's warm rays.

All at once, they heard the strangest noises coming
from the sack. They had never heard the sounds of Night
before, and it made them quake with fear.

"Let's throw it back into the river," said Hippopotamus.

"No, let's open it up and see what is inside," said Crocodile.

With that, he undid the knot with his sharp teeth and pulled
open the heavy sack.

Whooosh!

Out rushed the night insects – midges, moths, gnats and spiders.

Whooosh!

Out rushed the night birds – owls, jars and nightingales.

Whooosh!

Out rushed the night animals –
leopards, lions, bats and bullfrogs.

All these night creatures terrified Crocodile and Hippopotamus.
They dived deep into the muddy waters, then reappeared
in mid-river with just their eyes and noses above the swell.

Aje was waiting on the bank, sheltering beneath a leafy palm. The moment she saw the swarms of insects, flocks of birds and herds of animals, she uttered a low cry.

All at once, the spirits of Night grew calm, and a hush
descended on the land. The gentle hum of insects spread
throughout the bush. Twinkling stars gazed down from
a dark blue sky, and moonbeams trod a silvery path across
the waves. Owls hovered above woodland glades and leopard
eyes gleamed behind the trees. The cool air grew fragrant
with the scent of Night; a murmuring breeze rustled the
forest leaves.

Aje smiled. Now she knew she would find peace in her
husband's land, and she fell into a deep sleep.

When she awoke, Aje gave her new home special gifts.

To the brightest star shining in the sky, she said,
"You shall be Morning Star, announcing the birth
of each new day."

To the cockerel crowing on the wattle fence, she said,
"You shall be guardian of Night, warning us when
day is breaking."

To the birds chirruping all about her, she said,
"You shall sing most sweetly
at dawn, waking people with
your song."

And ever since then,
Morning Star, the cockerel
and the birds all announce
the coming of each new day.
But only after the restful
sleep of Night.

OTHER PICTURE BOOKS IN PAPERBACK FROM FRANCES LINCOLN

GROWING PAINS
Jenny Stow

Poor baby Shukudu! It's hard trying to be a rhinoceros when you have no horns.
."Horns take time to grow," says his mother. How Shukudu learns patience
and gains his heart's desire is portrayed with warmth and humour.

Suitable for National Curriculum English - Reading, Key Stage 1
Scottish Guidelines English Language - Reading, Levels B and C
ISBN 0-7112-1036-5 £4.99

THE FIRE CHILDREN
Eric Maddern
Illustrated by Frané Lessac

Why are some people black, some white, and others yellow, pink or brown?
This delightful West African creation myth tells how the first spirit-people
solve their loneliness using clay and fire – and fill the Earth with children
of every colour under the sun!

Suitable for National Curriculum English - Reading, Key Stages 1 and 2
Scottish Guidelines English Language - Reading, Levels B and C; Environmental Studies, Level C
ISBN 0-7112-0885-9 £4.99

RAINBOW BIRD
Eric Maddern
Illustrated by Adrienne Kennaway

"I'm boss for Fire," growls rough, tough Crocodile Man, and he keeps the rest
of the world cold and dark – until one day clever Bird Woman sees her opportunity
and seizes it. A North Australian Aboriginal fire myth that will warm
the hearts of adults and children alike.

Suitable for National Curriculum English - Reading, Key Stage 1
Scottish Guidelines English Language - Reading, Levels A and B
ISBN 0-7112-0898-0 £4.99

Frances Lincoln titles are available from all good bookshops.
Prices are correct at time of publication, but may be subject to change.